# DUCK

Based on *The Railway Series* by the Rev. W. Awdry

Illustrations by
*Robin Davies and Creative Design*

EGMONT

# EGMONT

*We bring stories to life*

First published in Great Britain 2005
by Egmont Books Limited
239 Kensington High Street, London W8 6SA
All Rights Reserved

Thomas the Tank Engine & Friends

A BRITT ALLCROFT COMPANY PRODUCTION

Based on The Railway Series by The Rev W Awdry

© Gullane (Thomas) LLC 2005

ISBN 1 4052 1713 8
1 3 5 7 9 10 8 6 4 2
Printed in China

*This* is a story about Duck the Great Western Engine. When he came to the station, he soon made it clear that he wouldn't put up with any nonsense. But there was one engine who was more than a match for him …

One morning, Percy was talking to Gordon and James in the engine shed.

"The Fat Controller is getting a bigger engine to help me," said Percy, proudly.

"Nonsense!" said Gordon. "We don't need a bigger engine."

"You just need to work more and chatter less!" said James.

Percy sighed. "No one listens to me. They think I'm a silly little engine and order me about. I'll show them!" But he didn't know how.

Later that day, Percy brought some coaches to the station.

"Hello, Percy!" said The Fat Controller. "You look tired."

"Yes, Sir," replied Percy, sadly. "I don't know if I'm standing on my dome or my wheels."

"Cheer up, Percy!" laughed The Fat Controller. "The new engine can do the work here alone. You can help Thomas and Toby build my new harbour."

"Oh, thank you, Sir," said Percy, happily.

The next morning, the new engine arrived. He was a Great Western Engine.

"What's your name?" asked The Fat Controller.

"Montague, Sir. But everyone calls me 'Duck' because they say I waddle," replied the engine. "I don't really, Sir. But I like being called Duck."

"Duck it is then!" said The Fat Controller. "Percy, come and show Duck around."

Percy and Duck got on well. Duck knew how to make the trucks behave and soon they were almost finished.

James, Gordon and Henry watched Duck quietly doing his work.

"Let's have some fun!" they whispered. And they wheeshed, "Quack! Quack! Quack!"

Percy was cross, but Duck ignored them. Then the engines began to order him about.

"Do they tell you to do things, Percy?" asked Duck.

"Yes, they do," replied Percy, sadly.

"Right," said Duck, "we'll soon stop that nonsense!" And he whispered something to Percy. "We'll do it tonight."

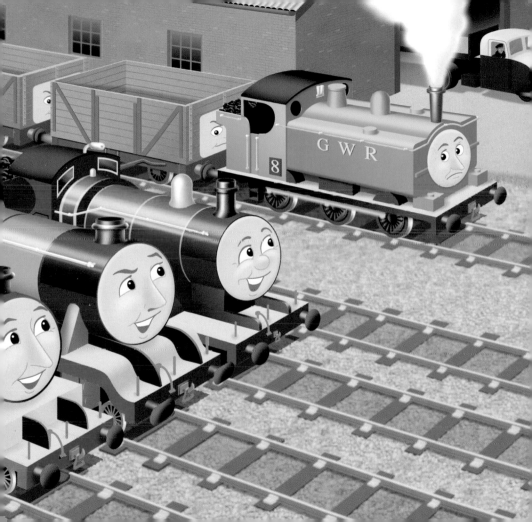

That evening, The Fat Controller was just about to go home for tea when he heard a terrible noise. He hurried to the yard.

Henry, Gordon and James were wheeshing furiously.

"Stop that noise!" bellowed The Fat Controller.

"They won't let us in," hissed Gordon.

And The Fat Controller realized that Duck and Perc were sat calmly at the points outside the engine shed, refusing to move.

The Fat Controller was very angry. "Duck, explain this behaviour!" he shouted.

"Beg your pardon, Sir," said Duck, politely. "But these engines are giving us orders. Please can you inform them that we only take orders from you."

"Duck and Percy, you are causing a disturbance!" thundered The Fat Controller. "And as for you," he said, turning to the big engines, "you made the disturbance! Duck is quite right. This is my Railway and I give the orders."

Henry, Gordon and James were very embarrassed.

From then on, Duck worked well at the yard and The Fat Controller was very pleased with him.

One day, Duck was resting in the engine shed when The Fat Controller arrived.

"Would you like to have a branch line of your own?" he asked.

"Yes, please, Sir," Duck replied, excitedly. And he took charge of his own branch line, which ran along the coast to the Small Railway.

Duck was very proud of his branch line. But he couldn't do all the work himself, so Donald and Douglas took turns to help him. One evening, he was talking to Donald.

"You don't understand how much The Fat Controller relies on me," said Duck, proudly. "I'm a Great Western and …"

"Quack, quack, quack," interrupted Donald. "Ye sound like ye laid an egg. Now let an engine sleep.

"Quack yourself," said Duck, indignantly.

The following morning, Duck spoke to his Driver.

"Donald says I quack as if I laid an egg," he said. "Let's play a joke on him to teach him a lesson."

"I have an idea!" laughed his Fireman, and he whispered something to Duck and his Driver.

That night, when Donald was asleep, Duck's Driver and Fireman put something into Donald's water tank.

The next morning, when Donald stopped for water, he found an unexpected passenger aboard. A little duckling popped out of his water tank! His Driver and Fireman could hardly believe their eyes, but Donald smiled.

"I know who's behind this," he laughed, and Donald told them what had happened in the shed.

The duckling was tame. She shared the Driver and Fireman's sandwiches and rode in the tender. But as the day went on, she grew tired of travelling and hopped off at a station, where she stayed.

Before they reached home, Donald and his Driver and Fireman made a plan. That night they were very busy. And when Duck's crew arrived in the morning, they made a surprise discovery!

"Look, Duck," they laughed. "There's a nest with an egg in it under your bunker!"

Donald opened a sleepy eye. "Well, well," he exclaimed, "you must have laid it in the night!"

Duck laughed, "You win, Donald. It would take a clever engine to get the better of you!"

Duck and Donald became good friends. And the duckling settled at the station. She lived in a pond nearby, but she always flew back to the station to welcome the engines. Donald was her favourite, and she sometimes hopped on for a ride. The Stationmaster called her Dilly, but to everyone else she was always Donald's Duck!

**The Thomas Story Library is THE definitive collection of stories about Thomas and ALL his Friends.**

You can buy the Collector's Pack
containing the first ten books for £24.99!

ISBN 1 4052 0827 9

5 more Thomas Story Library titles will be chuffing
into your local bookshop in September 2005:

**Trevor**
**Bertie**
**Diesel**
**Daisy**
**Spencer**

And there are even more
Thomas Story Library books to follow later!
**So go on, start your Thomas Story Library NOW!**